Jannie, Bobby, Tammy, Sara
Ian, Leslie, Hank, Terri
Nancy, Omar, Audrey, Chris, Miss Colman
Karen, Hannie, Ricky, Natalie

Scholastic Children's Books,
Commonwealth House, 1–19 New Oxford Street,
London WC1A 1NU, UK
a division of Scholastic Ltd
London ~ New York ~ Toronto ~ Sydney ~ Auckland

First published in the US by Scholastic Inc., 1997
First published in the UK by Scholastic Ltd, 1997

ISBN 0 590 19472 0

Typeset by Rowland Phototypesetting Ltd,
Bury St Edmunds, Suffolk
Printed by Cox & Wyman Ltd, Reading, Berks.

10 9 8 7 6 5 4 3 2 1

2 A

STONEYBROOK
ACADEMY

THE KIDS IN·
MISS COLMAN'S CLASS

5·
TWIN TROUBLE

ANN M. MARTIN

Illustrated by Charles Tang

Hippo

*This book is for
Elizabeth Strutton*

Terri and Tammy

Terri Barkan was a twin – an identical twin – and she liked it. She could not imagine anything so boring as having just an ordinary old brother or sister. Or worse, no brother or sister at all. Terri liked being just the same as Tammy. Samesies.

"Girls!" the twins' father called up the stairs. "What do you want for supper tonight? Pasta or chicken?"

"Pasta, please!" Terri called back.

At the same time, from the next bedroom, Tammy called, "Pasta, please!"

"Jinx!" cried Terri, and she ran into her

1

sister's room. "Samesies! Same words, same time."

The twins were always saying the same thing at the same time.

Terri was seven years old. Tammy was the same age as Terri, minus one hour. "I was born first. I am the big sister," Terri used to boast. That was when the twins were five. Now, being an hour older or younger did not seem to matter much.

Terri eyed the clothes lying on her sister's bed. "Is that what you are going to wear to school tomorrow?" she asked.

"Yep," replied Tammy.

"Hmm. I was going to wear my fish sweater, too. Maybe I will change to my striped sweater. We just dressed samesies on Friday."

For a long time, Terri and her sister had dressed alike every single day. But in first grade, their classmates had started to call both of them Twinny instead of Terri or Tammy. That was too much sameness. Now they usually dressed differently, at least at school.

"We do not want to drive Miss Colman crazy," Terri had said to Tammy at the beginning of the year.

"No," agreed Tammy.

Miss Colman was the twins' best teacher ever. In fact, she was the favourite teacher of most of her second-graders. She thought up fun projects, she smiled a lot, she almost never shouted and she hardly ever got angry. Also, she was fair and honest.

"Pasta time!" called Mr Barkan from downstairs.

"I will have to choose my outfit later," said Terri. "Come on."

The girls ran downstairs to the kitchen. They sat at the table with their parents. When the pasta had been served, Terri said, "Did you know that Ian's mother is going to have a baby?"

"Mrs Johnson?" said Terri's mother. "How nice for Ian's family."

3

"Mum?" said Tammy. "Do you think we will have another baby?"

Mr and Mrs Barkan glanced at each other. "Probably not," replied Mrs Barkan. "We think two kids are just right. But you never know."

Terri thought two kids were just right, too. She did want a pet, though. She and Tammy had had a frog once. Frank. But Terri wanted a dog. Or a cat. Still, she thought her family was pretty nice the way it was. A mum, a dad and two samesies.

That night, Terri finally decided to wear the striped sweater. And jeans, since Tammy was wearing leggings. Then she and Tammy played Scrabble Junior.

"I won!" cried Terri.

"I won last time," said Tammy.

"And I got the same score you did when you won."

The twins grinned at each other. Then they began another game. They played Scrabble until it was bedtime.

School

Terri and Tammy hurried along the corridor of Stoneybrook Academy. They paused when they reached the doorway to Room 2A. Then they stood side by side and entered the room together.

"Hi, Terri! Hi, Tammy!" called Karen Brewer.

"Hi, Karen!" said the twins.

Karen was sitting on her desk in the back row. Nancy Dawes was standing in front of her. Karen was plaiting Nancy's hair. Next to Nancy, Hannie Papadakis was waiting patiently for Karen to plait her hair. Karen, Nancy and Hannie were best friends. They called themselves the Three Musketeers.

6

Terri and Tammy put their coats in the cloakroom. Then they put their things in their desks. Terri wished that her desk was next to Tammy's, but it was not. Miss Colman had seated the kids where she wanted them, and that was that. So Terri sat at one end of the third row, and Tammy sat one row up and two seats along. Oh, well. At least the twins could see each other easily. Sometimes they even passed notes.

Terri looked around the class. She wanted to see who else was there. She pretended she was taking the register.

OK. Over in the reading corner were Sara Ford and Natalie Springer. Sara was new to Stoneybrook Academy, and Terri liked her very much. She was glad Miss Colman had seated Sara next to her. (Otherwise, Terri might have been surrounded by boys. Ricky Torres sat behind her, and Chris Lamar sat in front of her.) Natalie Springer was sloppy and messy, but Terri liked her, too. She had known Natalie since kindergarten.

7

At the back of the room, Leslie Morris and Jannie Gilbert were playing with Hootie, the class guinea pig. Leslie and Jannie were best friends – and they were the best enemies of Karen, Nancy and Hannie.

Terri heard a crash then. She looked towards the door of the classroom. Of course I just heard a crash, she thought. The boys have arrived. There were sixteen kids in Miss Colman's class. Ten girls and six boys. Four of the boys had just arrived in a big, noisy group. Chris and Ricky, and Hank Ruebens and Bobby Gianelli. Terri did not mind Chris, Ricky or Hank. But Bobby . . . well, Bobby was a bully. Sometimes Terri was afraid of him.

Then another boy entered the room. Omar Harris. Omar was OK. He had a sheepdog named Buster. Omar was followed – very quietly – by Ian Johnson. Terri liked Ian, too. Ian's hobby was reading. The last kid to arrive was Audrey Green. Audrey hung her coat in the cloakroom, then peered into Mr Berger's room next door. Mr Berger was the other second-grade teacher. In the mornings, the door between his room and Miss Colman's room was always open. Mr Berger kept an eye on all the kids until Miss Colman arrived.

"Hey, Terri," said Tammy. "Come here."

"Why?"

"Let's play cat's cradle."

"OK."

Terri took her cat's cradle string to Tammy's desk.

"I can show you something new," said Audrey. She hurried across the room to the twins.

"Cool," said Terri and Tammy.

"Jinx!" cried Tammy.

"Good morning, class," said Miss Colman.

Terri looked up. Their teacher had arrived. She put the string in her pocket. Cat's cradle would have to wait.

3
The Readathon

Miss Colman took the register. "Everyone is here," she said. "That is good, because I have an announcement to make. I would like all of you to hear it."

Terri wriggled in her seat. This sounded interesting.

"Our school," Miss Colman began, "is about to start an exciting project. How many of you know Burger Town?"

Terri raised her hand. So did Tammy. So did almost every kid in the classroom. They had eaten plenty of hamburger meals at Burger Town. It was one of Terri's favourite restaurants.

Miss Colman smiled. "I thought so. Well,

the people at Burger Town have come up with a very generous offer. They have told our school, and several other schools, that they would like to run readathons to help our libraries. They said that for every one thousand pages the pupils read, they will give the school a hundred dollars to buy books and materials for the library."

Terri slumped in her seat. And Bobby Gianelli said just what she had been thinking. "A *thousand* pages? Miss Colman, I cannot read a thousand pages!"

"Oh, no. Of course not, Bobby. That is not what I meant," said Miss Colman. "Nobody has to read a thousand pages alone. We will work together. Every pupil in the school. You read as many pages as you can. All the pages will be added together. With so many kids reading, we will read thousands and thousands of pages. But you just read as many as you can. You will see."

"How much time will we have to do the reading in?" asked Tammy.

"A month," replied Miss Colman. "Let

me explain. Starting today, every pupil in every class in our school will read books for the readathon. You may choose any books you like. Each time you finish reading a book, let me know. I will ask you a few questions about it so I know you understood it. If you can answer the questions, then the book counts for the readathon. I will mark down the number of pages in the book. The next time you finish a book, I will add those pages to

the ones you have already read."

"Can we read short books?" asked Audrey.

"Certainly," replied Miss Colman. "But you will not earn as many pages for them."

"Can we read at home?" asked Karen Brewer.

"Yes," said Miss Colman. "I will give you half an hour to read in school every day, too. But you will probably do most of your reading at home. Just tell me each time you finish a book, all right?" The kids in Miss

Colman's class nodded. "Another thing," she went on. "At the end of each day, the teachers will add up all the new pages their pupils have read. Then they will add the new pages together to see how many pages all the pupils in the school have read. We will keep track of the pages out in the corridor, where everyone can see. Our art teacher is making a big paper caterpillar for us. Each time we read two hundred and fifty more pages, another link will be added to the caterpillar's body. We can watch our caterpillar grow.

"And next month, someone from Burger Town will come to our school. He will give us a cheque for the pages we have read. He will also give a prize to the class who have read the most pages, and to the pupil in each class who has read the most pages."

"Cool!" exclaimed Ian.

"*Very* cool," agreed Sara.

And Terri passed a note to Tammy that said, "Let's read the books in the Becky Morton series."

4

Reading Fever

After break that day, Miss Colman said, "OK, class. For the next month, we will have half an hour reading every day at this time. Now is your chance to start reading for the readathon. You may choose books from our classroom library. If you have a book from home or from the public library, that is fine, too. If you want to go to the school library now, you may go with Mr Berger. He is taking some of his pupils there."

Four kids went off with Mr Berger. But Terri and Tammy and the others stayed behind. Terri and Tammy made a dash for the bookshelf in the reading corner. Quite a few Becky Morton books were there. They were the twins' favourites. They were stories about the adventures of Becky Morton, a girl their age who lived in colonial America, hundreds of years ago.

Terri chose a book called *Becky Morton Rides Again*. She carried it to her desk. She opened it on the last page. The number on the page was 63. Wow! thought Terri. When I finish this book, I will have read sixty-three pages.

Terri flipped to the front of the book. She began to read. She read and read and read. She forgot about her classroom and the other kids and even the readathon. So she was quite surprised to hear Miss Colman say, "All right, class. I am afraid you must put your books away. The half hour is over."

Terri blinked. The half hour had felt like five minutes. She checked to see what page she was on. Twenty-four. She had read three chapters and part of a fourth. She leaned across Sara's desk and called softly, "Tammy? Tammy?"

Tammy turned around. "Yes?"

"How many pages did you read?"

"Forty-one. How many did you read?"

"Forty-one? I read, um, twenty-four."

Now that was odd. Terri and Tammy were almost always samesies. They did everything the same. Hmm.

At the end of the day, Miss Colman said, "Did anyone finish a book today? I can ask you some questions."

No one had. Not on the first day of the readathon. But at the end of the second day, four kids had finished books. Miss Colman quizzed them on the stories. Then she announced, "Excellent! Ian has earned forty-seven pages, Karen has earned forty-five, Sara has earned fifty-five and Tammy has earned forty-six."

Out in the corridor, on the other side of the school, the caterpillar's head had been taped to the wall. It was a friendly caterpillar with eyes made of cotton wool balls, and antennae that really bobbed. On Tuesday afternoon, the teachers attached a round red link to the head. The kids at Stoneybrook Academy had read their first 250 pages. The caterpillar had started to grow.

Terri and Tammy read the Becky Morton books all week. On Wednesday, Terri finally finished *Becky Morton Rides Again*. Tammy had finished *Becky Morton and the Dirty Dozen* and was halfway through *Becky Morton and the New Baby*. By Thursday afternoon, Tammy had finished *Becky Morton and the New Baby*, her second book of the week. She thought she would finish a third book by Friday afternoon.

"Your *third*?!" exclaimed Terri. Terri was not sure she would finish her second. She did not mind that so much, but she did mind being so different from Tammy. Something felt wrong.

5
Star Reader

The caterpillar was in a corridor on the opposite side of the building from Miss Colman's room. Terri did not get to see it often. She and Tammy had peeked at it on Tuesday to see what it looked like. Now, on Friday, Terri wondered how much it had grown. She thought another link or two might have been added.

"Let's go and look at the caterpillar, Tammy," said Terri as the girls ran into school that morning.

Tammy grinned. "OK." Then she said, "Hey, Terri, I know what kind of caterpillar it is."

"You do?"

"Yep. It is a bookworm. Get it?"

Terri grinned, too. "Yes. A book—"

Terri stopped speaking. She stopped walking, too. She had turned a corner in the corridor, and now she was simply staring.

"Terri? What is—" Tammy started to say. Then she stopped talking, too. She was looking at what Terri had seen. "Wow!" she said. "Wow . . . Oh, my gosh. . ."

It was the caterpillar. A lot of other kids were looking at it, too. The last time the twins had seen it, it had had a head and one round body piece. Now, the caterpillar stretched halfway down the corridor. Terri could not believe it.

"Come on. Let's count," she said to Tammy. "Let's see how long it is." Terri and Tammy started counting with the red piece. "One, two, three, four," they began. A few minutes later they were still counting. "Eighty-six, eighty-seven, eighty-eight."

"Eighty-*eight*!" cried Tammy.

"And each piece stands for two hundred

and fifty pages," said Terri. "How many is that all together?"

A fifth-grade girl was standing nearby. She was holding a calculator. "Twenty-two thousand," she announced.

"Twenty-two *thousand*? That must be wrong," said Terri.

"Nope." The girl shook her head. "There are two hundred and thirty kids at Stoneybrook Academy. If each kid read about ninety-five pages this week . . . yep, that would work out."

"Wow! Amazing!" whispered Terri.

The caterpillar was all the kids in Miss Colman's class could talk about that morning.

"Did you see it? It is *so long*!" exclaimed Jannie.

"I read over a hundred pages this week," said Karen.

"I read eighty-nine," said Sara.

"I am going to finish my third book today," said Tammy.

Terri did not say anything. She had not even finished the second Becky Morton book.

"Class," said Miss Colman later that morning, "I am very proud of you. You have done lots of reading this week."

"Did you see the caterpillar?" Karen asked Miss Colman. "It has eighty-eight links. That is ginormous."

"It certainly is," agreed Miss Colman. "And do you know what? Our class is

responsible for almost *four* of those links. You have read nine hundred and sixty pages altogether this week. And three of you have been *star* readers. Karen, Ian and Tammy, each of you read more than one hundred pages since Monday. Congratulations!"

The kids in Miss Colman's class clapped politely.

Terri clapped along with them. But she did not feel very happy. She did not

exactly feel sad, either. She just felt confused.

She was not used to being so different from Tammy.

6

Samesies

Terri made a decision. She was going to spend as much time as possible reading over the weekend. She would have Friday afternoon and then two whole days for nothing but reading. Maybe, she thought, if she just had more time, she could read as many books as Tammy.

So on Friday, as soon as she got home from school, Terri settled down with *Becky Morton and the Dirty Dozen.* She read until dinnertime. After dinner, she read until bedtime. She finished *Becky Morton and the Dirty Dozen.*

"Yes!" cried Terri.

On Saturday morning – first thing – Terri

began *Becky Morton and the New Baby*. By bedtime that night, she had finished it.

"Yes!" she cried again.

On Sunday morning, Terri decided she was a little tired of Becky Morton. She she started a book called *Fantastic Mr Fox*, by Roald Dahl. By suppertime, she had finished it.

"Tammy, Tammy! I finished *two* and a *half* books this weekend! Isn't that great? That is a record for me! How many books did you read?" (Tammy had been reading all weekend, too.)

"Well, um. . ." Tammy began. "Um, I read five and a half books." Tammy looked sorry. "I did not mean to. I was just reading along, and before I knew it. . ."

"That is OK," said Terri slowly. "You should not apologize. We are supposed to read as much as we can. The more we read, the more money our library will get."

"But still," said Tammy.

"I know," said Terri.

"What happened to us?" asked Tammy. "Why aren't we samesies?"

Terri shook her head. "I don't know."

"Maybe we can be samesies again," said Tammy.

"How?"

"Well, I could try to slow down. I do not *have* to read so fast." Tammy did not sound very excited about her idea.

"No. Do not do that," said Terri. "Then you will not earn as many pages." Terri thought for a moment. "I know! I could try to speed up. I will just read really, really fast."

Tammy looked interested. "Can you do that?"

"Sure. Why not? I will just let my eyes zip along the pages like a bee. It should be easy. I bet I could read a whole book by tomorrow. Well, maybe by Tuesday."

Tammy smiled. "Cool."

"It feels funny to be different, doesn't it?" said Terri. "I mean, we are still different. If I have to read really fast to keep up with you, it means I am slower. So we are different. Not samesies."

"Yes," said Tammy.

"I know. Let's wear the same outfits tomorrow," suggested Terri. "Like we used to do every day."

"OK."

The girls looked through their wardrobes. They decided to wear their jean skirts and purple heart sweaters with tights and their red shoes.

Fantastic Mr. F
Roald Dah

"Remember, we have to do our hair the same, too," said Tammy.

The girls decided on ponytails.

That night, Terri lay in her bed, thinking. She was pleased about the matching outfits. But when she thought about the reading, she got a funny feeling in the pit of her stomach.

7

School Choir

"Class," said Miss Colman the next morning, "I have something exciting to tell you. Our school is going to have its very own choir. Mr Saffron is going to be in charge of it." (Mr Saffron was one of the music teachers.) "We have never had a choir before. This will be our first. And Mr Saffron said that anybody can audition for it. So if you are interested, go to the music room after lunch today, instead of going to the playground for break."

"If we join the choir will we always miss break?" asked Jannie.

Miss Colman shook her head. "No. Just today. Mr Saffron said the choir is going to meet after school." She looked around the classroom. "Is any one of you interested?"

Terri was. She started to raise her hand. Then she stopped. She looked at Tammy. Would Tammy raise her hand, too?

Tammy turned around. She glanced at Terri. The twins nodded at each other. Then they raised their hands.

"Very good," said Miss Colman. "Ian, Omar, Jannie and our twins. I see you are dressed alike today, girls," she added.

"But we wore different ribbons in our hair," said Tammy.

"So you can tell us apart," said Terri.

Miss Colman smiled. "That was very thoughtful of you."

After lunch that day, Miss Colman walked Jannie, Omar, Ian and the twins to the music room. She left them with Mr Saffron, and a lot of other kids.

"Are *all* these kids trying out for the choir?" Tammy whispered.

"I guess so," Terri whispered back. "There are so many of them."

Mr Saffron clapped his hands. "Greetings," he said. "Thank you for coming. I am Mr Saffron. As you know, Stoneybrook Academy is about to have its first choir. I would like thirty or so of you to be in it. That means, unfortunately, that some of you who audition today will not get to be part of the choir. If you are not chosen, please do not feel too bad. We will have auditions every year. So you can try again next year.

"Now, to begin, I would like to hear you sing in small groups." Mr Saffron counted the kids in the room. "Groups of five, I think."

Terri and Tammy waited patiently for Mr Saffron to call their names. When he did, they stood up along with three other kids. Mr Saffron wrote their names on a sheet of paper.

"OK, listen for the scales," he said.

Just as all the other kids had done, Terri

listened to Mrs Dade (another music teacher) play a scale on the piano.

"Now let me hear you sing that as a group," said Mr Saffron.

"Ah, ah, ah, ah, ah, ah, ah, ah," sang Terri and the others.

"Very nice," said Mr Saffron. "Now one at a time. Terri?"

"Ah, ah, ah, ah, ah, ah, ah, ah."

"Great. Tammy?"

"Ah, ah, ah, ah, ah, ah, ah, ah."

"Wonderful."

Mr Saffron listened to each of the kids. Sometimes he asked two or three of them to sing together. Sometimes he wanted to hear someone alone for a second time and even a third time.

"I will make my decisions by the end of the day," Mr Saffron told the kids as they were leaving.

Terri could not wait. At the end of the day, when she heard Mr Saffron's voice on the loudspeaker, her heart began to beat faster. And then she heard him say her name – and Tammy's and Omar's.

"Yes!" cried Terri. She and Tammy were samesies again.

Terri's Secret Plan

On Tuesday, the twins dressed alike again. They did their hair the same way, too. They helpfully wore different coloured hairslides, though. Blue for Terri, red for Tammy.

Even so, Bobby Gianelli said, "Hey, I am seeing double!" when he saw them. "I'd better go to the opticians."

And Hannie called them Twinny.

"I am *Terri*," said Terri crossly.

"And I am Tammy. See my hairslide?"

"I cannot be bothered to look at hairslides all the time," said Jannie.

"She is just cross because Mr Saffron did not pick her for the choir," Terri whispered to Tammy.

"Bad loser," Tammy muttered.

"Do not pay attention to her," said Terri. "*I* am not going to. I am going to finish *Becky Morton and the Snowstorm* now. I started it last night and I read really fast. I bet I can finish it by the time Miss Colman gets here."

Sure enough, Terri was reading the words "The End" when she heard Miss Colman say, "Good morning, class."

Terri snapped the book shut. Done! She could not wait until the end of the day.

"Miss Colman, Miss Colman! I finished another book," Terri announced as soon as the last bell had rung.

"My goodness. Already?" replied Miss Colman. "That was fast."

Terri nodded. "Yep."

"OK. Which book?"

Terri was standing by Miss Colman's desk. "This one," she said. She handed her *Becky Morton and the Snowstorm*.

"Oh. This is a good one, isn't it?"

"Yes," replied Terri. Although, when she

37

thought about it, she could not remember much about what had happened.

"All right. Let me see," began Miss Colman. She flipped some pages in the book. "OK. Before the storm begins, what gift does Becky give to Mr O'Toole?"

"Gift?" repeated Terri. "To Mr O'Toole?"

"Yes. In his shop."

"In his shop?"

"In the butcher's shop?" Miss Colman added helpfully.

"Well, um . . . I – I do not exactly remember." In fact, Terri did not even remember anyone in the story named Mr O'Toole.

Miss Colman glanced down at a sheet of paper on her desk. Terri glanced at it, too. She saw her classmates' names in a list on the left side of the page. Next to each name, in pencil, was a number. A lot of the numbers looked as if they had been rubbed out quite a few times.

"Is that where you write down our page numbers?" Terri asked.

Miss Colman nodded. Then she said, "Can you answer the question?" Terri shook her head, so Miss Colman said, "OK. Let's try another. What happens to the new baby during the story?"

Terri frowned. "Does she . . . get ill?"

"No," said Miss Colman. Then she added, "I am sorry, Terri. I think maybe you read a little too fast. I am afraid I cannot count these pages. You may try reading the book again. Or you may go on and read a different book."

Terri hung her head. She had wanted Miss Colman to add 61 to the number by Terri's name on the sheet. But Miss Colman would not do it.

Terri felt cross. But then she got a sneaky idea for a secret plan.

Sneaking
Around

"Tammy?" said Terri. "What gift does Becky give Mr O'Toole in *Becky Morton and the Snowstorm*?"

"A cake," replied Tammy. "Why?"

It was the next morning. Terri and Tammy, dressed in matching jumpers and leggings, walked slowly down the corridor towards classroom 2A.

Terri shrugged. "I just could not remember," she said. "Um, Tammy? Who is Mr O'Toole? Is he a butcher?"

"Well, he works in a butcher's shop. But he is not a butcher. He just helps out. And

41

he and Becky get to be friends. Terri?"

"Yes?"

"How fast did you read the book?"

"A little too fast," Terri admitted. She thought about asking Tammy what had happened to the baby during the snowstorm, but she decided not to bother. She was too busy thinking about her sneaky plan. She was going to carry it out as soon as lunch was over that day.

"Who wants to play hopscotch?" asked Tammy.

"Me!" cried Natalie and Sara. They began to empty their lunch trays.

"I have to go to the toilet." said Terri. "I will come outside later."

Terri hurried out of the canteen. Her heart began to pound. It was time to put her plan into action.

She walked down the corridor. She walked quickly by the girls' toilets. She walked straight to classroom 2A. Terri paused outside the doorway. She peeped inside. (She was holding her breath.) Good. The room was empty.

Terri tiptoed inside. She looked around. She was not sure she had ever been all alone in 2A before. Her heart began to pound even faster. Terri ran over to Miss Colman's desk. The first thing she saw was the sheet of paper with the names listed on it. Perfect.

Terri reached for the paper. She looked at the number next to her name. It was one of the lowest numbers on the sheet.

Tammy's was one of the highest. It had been rubbed out lots of times. That was because Tammy kept finishing books, so Miss Colman kept adding to the number of pages.

Terri picked up a pencil. Carefully she rubbed out the number by her name. She thought for a moment. Then she wrote down a number that was almost as big as Tammy's. She rubbed it out. She wrote the same number as Tammy's.

"Ahem!" said a voice from behind Terri.

Terri jumped. She dropped the pencil. She turned around.

Miss Colman was peering over her shoulder.

Cheating

"Terri? What are you doing?" asked Miss Colman. Miss Colman was not smiling. In fact, she was frowning.

"I was – I was—" Terri started to say.

Miss Colman took the paper from Terri. She frowned harder. "Terri, the last time I looked, you had read about half the number of pages I see written here. And this number is not in my handwriting."

"I know, I know," said Terri. "I just – I changed it." Terri could feel a tear starting to slide down her cheek.

"But why?" asked Miss Colman. "You have been doing a lot of reading, Terri. You have been working hard."

"I wanted to be the same as Tammy," Terri managed to say. "Look. See how many pages Tammy has read?"

"Why do you want to be the same?"

"Because we are always the same. Samesies."

"You are not *exactly* the same," Miss Colman said.

"Yes, we are," said Terri.

Miss Colman sighed. "No, you are not. And anyway, that is not the point. The point is that you were cheating."

"Well," said Terry. She looked down at her feet. "Um, well. . ."

"You know you were cheating, don't you?" said Miss Colman.

"Yes," whispered Terri.

"All right. Terri, I want you to know that I am not angry with you. But I am very, *very* disappointed in you. I thought I could trust you. Now I am not sure. You sneaked in here to do something behind my back. And you took something private off my desk. Do you know that these things were wrong?"

"Yes," whispered Terri again.

Miss Colman looked at her watch. "Lunch break will not be over for a while," she said. "So we have time to go to the office. Please come along with me now."

"To the head's office?" Terri gasped.

"Yes, but not to see the head," said Miss Colman. "I want to phone your parents." She held out her hand to Terri.

Terri took her teacher's hand. She walked with her to the office.

"My parents are both at work," Terri told Miss Colman.

Miss Colman nodded. She looked up the Barkans' work numbers. She dialled Mrs Barkan first. Mrs Barkan was in a meeting. Miss Colman called Mr Barkan next.

Terri listened while Miss Colman told Mr Barkan what Terri had done. She could feel her face going red. After a few minutes, Miss Colman handed the phone to Terri.

"Terri," said her father," I am very disappointed in you."

"So is Miss Colman," Terri managed to say.

"We will have a talk tonight."

"OK," said Terri.

That night, as soon as Mr and Mrs Barkan returned from work, they sat down in the front room with Terri. Terri tried hard not to cry. She had been trying not to cry all afternoon.

"Terri," said her mother, "your father told me about Miss Colman's call today. You understand that we have to punish you, don't you?"

"Yes," replied Terri.

She waited to hear what her punishment would be.

Good News

"We were going to tell you that you may not take part in the readathon," said Mrs Barkan. "But we are not going to do that. Reading is much, much too important. Instead, you may not watch any television for two weeks."

"OK," murmured Terri. Two weeks was a very long time, but she did not say so. She was glad that she could still be in the readathon.

"Now," said Mr Barkan, "when Miss Colman called today, she said something about you and Tammy not being samesies. What is that all about? I mean, why did that make you want to cheat?"

Terri tried to explain.

The Barkans called Tammy into the front room.

"Does this bother you, too?" they asked her. "Not being samesies all the time?"

"Yes," admitted Tammy.

"Hmm," said Mrs Barkan. "I believe it is time to ask Grandma Doris to come for a visit. I will call her tonight."

Terri looked at Tammy. The twins frowned. Grandma Doris? They had not seen her since they were four. Why was their mother going to ask her to visit? And what did she have to do with the readathon?

Although Terri was confused, she began to feel better. And then better and better. First of all, no TV for two weeks was a big punishment, but it was not *so* bad. And second of all, when Mrs Barkan called Grandma Doris, Grandma Doris said she wanted to come and visit right away. She was going to fly to Connecticut on Saturday and stay for two whole weeks. Very excit-

50

ing. The twins planned to decorate the guest room for her.

Then when Terri and Tammy arrived at school the next day, they decided to check on the caterpillar. "Let's see how long he is," said Terri. "I wonder if he has grown."

"Hey, wait!" exclaimed Tammy. "What is the caterpillar doing in *this* corridor? He was not here before."

Terri saw that the caterpillar stretched halfway down the corridor they were standing in. The twins ran to the corner. They peered around it. The caterpillar started at the end of the next corridor, ran all the way along the wall and turned the corner.

"Cool!" exclaimed Terri, and she felt even better.

At choir practice that afternoon, Mr Saffron had good news. "Guess what," he said. "Our choir has been asked to perform at the readathon assembly. The assembly will be very exciting. Our head is going to give a speech. Some of the fifth-graders are going to put on a short play, and we are going to sing several songs. *And*, one of you will sing a solo in each song. Do you know what a solo is?"

A fourth-grade boy raised his hand. "A solo is one person singing alone, isn't it?"

"Yes, it is," replied Mr Saffron. "Very good. We will be singing three songs so we will need three soloists. If you would like to audition for a solo part, stay after school tomorrow. The auditions will be held right here."

Terri grinned at Tammy. She flashed her the thumbs-up sign. As soon as choir practice was over, Terri said, "Cool, Tammy! Auditions for solos! Let's both go for it, OK?"

"Definitely!" said Tammy.

"Let's practise singing this afternoon," Terri went on. "And tomorrow we will dress samesies for the auditions."

"OK," agreed Tammy.

Terri was grinning. Her bad day the day before had turned into a good day today.

12

Different Again

On Friday, the twins wore their red pinafore dresses and white blouses to school. They both wore white tights and black shoes. They did their hair in ponytails tied with red ribbons.

"Even our underwear is the same," said Terri proudly.

"Not a bit of difference," added Tammy.

By the time the bell rang at the end of the day, Terri's heart was beating fast. It felt like a bird flapping in her chest.

"Are you nervous?" she whispered to Tammy as they hurried down the corridor to the music room.

"Yes. Are you?"

"Yes."

The first thing Mr Saffron said to the kids who had gathered for the auditions was, "Do not be nervous."

But Terri could not help it.

Mr Saffron taught the kids a new song that day. It was called *Getting To Know You*. He asked them to sing it as a group. Then he asked each of them to sing the first part of it alone.

Terri's heart began to pound again. But when Mr Saffron called on her, she sang nice and loudly. "Getting to know you, getting to know all about you. Getting to like you, getting to hope you like me."

"Very nice," said Mr Saffron. He smiled.

When Tammy sang, she sang nicely, but not so loudly. Mr Saffron smiled at her. But Terri noticed he did not say anything.

Eleven kids had shown up for the auditions. When each of them had had a chance to sing alone, Mr Saffron studied the notes he had been writing. He spoke to Mrs Dade. Finally he said, "OK. This was a tough

decision, but I have made my choices. Our soloists will be Max Lieb, Kate Gibbel and Terri Barkan."

Terri's mouth dropped open. She did not know whether to laugh or to cry. She had got a solo. But . . . why hadn't Tammy got one, too?

"We are different again," Terri said to Tammy.

"I know," replied Tammy, and she frowned at her twin.

13

Grandma Doris

Grandma Doris arrived at lunchtime on Saturday. She pulled up in front of the twins' house in a yellow taxi.

"A taxi!" Terri said with a gasp. No one had ever come to their house in a taxi. Terri and Tammy ran across the lawn.

Grandma Doris climbed out of the car. She hugged the twins. Terri noticed that she did not say, "Goodness, you have grown!" And she was pleased.

The driver opened the boot. He pulled out four large suitcases.

"Here you go," said Grandma Doris. She handed him some money.

"Why, *thank* you!" exclaimed the driver.

"Are those all yours?" Terri pointed to the suitcases. They were lined up on the pavement.

"Yes," replied Grandma Doris. "But they are not all clothes. One of them is full of presents."

"For *us*? A whole suitcase full of presents?"

"Well, I have not seen you in three years. Now, come along. Help me get all this stuff inside."

The taxi drove off. Terri began to drag one of the suitcases across the lawn. Tammy pulled another. Grandma Doris grabbed a third. Luckily, Mr and Mrs Barkan came outside then. After a lot of hugging and kissing, the suitcases were finally taken inside.

"Which one do you think is the one full of presents?" Tammy whispered to Terri.

"It is that one," Grandma Doris replied, pointing. Then she winked at Tammy. "I have the ears of a twenty-year-old," she said.

Terri gulped. She was not sure what to think of her grandmother.

After lunch that day, Grandma Doris handed out some of her presents. Terri got a sweat shirt from the University of Miami, a set of watercolour paints, a swimming costume and a stuffed dolphin. Tammy got a bead-stringing kit, three pairs of socks and two books.

"Why didn't she give us samesies?" Terri asked Tammy.

Tammy shrugged. She was reading one of her new books.

After dinner that night, Grandma Doris said, "Well, I have one present left for you girls." She hauled a large book out of the suitcase. Then she sat on the couch with the book on her lap. She patted the space on either side of her. "Come here. Sit down," she said. And Terri and Tammy curled up with her.

"These are pictures of me when I was your age," Grandma Doris said.

Terri peered at the old black-and-white photos. "Which one is you? You look exactly like that other girl."

"That other girl is your Great-aunt Martha."

Terri vaguely remembered her great-aunt. She had died when Terri was five. "How come you look so much alike?" she asked.

"Because we were twins, of course. Just like you two."

"*You* had a twin sister?" exclaimed Tammy.

"But how come you are dressed like that?" asked Terri, looking through the album.

"You mean dressed so differently?" said Grandma Doris. "Well, because we *were* different, of course. Martha was always the shy one, and I was the talker. I was very bold. Martha liked to dress up, and I liked music. You must take after me, by the way," Grandma Doris said to Terri.

"Well, I – I guess so." Terri hardly knew what to say. But she found herself grinning.

Tammy was grinning, too.

"Tell us more about you and Great-aunt Martha," said Terri. "Please."

Prize Day

Grandma Doris told quite a few stories about when she and Great-aunt Martha were little girls.

"Once," she said, "our Auntie Laura had come to take care of us for a week, and we told her I was Martha and Martha was me, and she believed us for two days. I went to Martha's drawing lesson, and Martha went to my piano lesson before anyone found out. It was Martha's horrible piano playing that gave us away," added Grandma Doris.

"Did you always do such different things?" Terri asked her. "Like, you taking piano and your sister taking drawing?"

"Oh, yes," said Grandma Doris. "Otherwise, we would have been bored silly. Things were much more exciting that way. We had different friends, too. Which meant that we had *more* friends, because I had all of mine, plus all of Martha's and vice versa."

Now *that*, thought Terri, was very interesting.

"I am doing really well in our readathon at school," Tammy told Grandma Doris.

"And I am going to sing a solo at our assembly," said Terri.

"How wonderful," said Grandma Doris. "I am proud of both of you."

Nine days later, Grandma Doris went home. Terri had enjoyed her visit very much. She was sorry to see her leave. But she did not feel sorry for long. She did not have time to feel sorry. It was the last week of the readathon. And it was almost time for the assembly – and for Terri's solo.

The caterpillar was now four *hundred* sections long. Terri was amazed. It took up almost two whole corridors.

"By the end of the week," Tammy said to Terri one morning, "three of those caterpillar parts will be mine."

"Three?" replied Terri. "How many pages is that?"

"Seven hundred and fifty." Tammy was grinning.

"That is great," said Terri. And she meant it. "I have only read two hundred and thirteen pages. But Grandma Doris said it was all right to be different."

"She said it was *good* to be different."

"Yep."

That was why Terri was wearing jeans that day, and Tammy was wearing a pinafore dress. They had not dressed alike in days.

On Thursday afternoon the next week, Terri went to the music room. She met Max Lieb and Kate Gibbel there. Mr Saffron had called a special rehearsal for the kids with solo parts. The readathon was over, and the assembly was going to be held the next day.

"You sound wonderful," Mr Saffron told the kids when the rehearsal was over. "All of you do. You will be just fine tomorrow. Remember, if you start to feel nervous, look at me, not at the audience."

I am not going to feel nervous, Terri thought.

But she was wrong.

When it was time for the assembly to begin the next morning, Terri felt butterflies in her stomach. She was standing on a block with Tammy and the rest of the choir. They were backstage in the assembly hall at Stoneybrook Academy, and the curtain was pulled closed in front of them. Terri knew what was on the other side of that curtain. The audience. All of the pupils and teachers, plus her parents and a lot of other parents.

Terri gulped. She clutched Tammy's hand.

The Long, Long Caterpillar

The assembly was going to open with a song by the choir. That was the very first thing the audience would hear. Thirty voices singing a song Terri liked very much called "Where Have All the Flowers Gone?"

Mr Saffron stepped in front of the choir. Behind him was the curtain. And on the other side of the curtain was the audience.

Mr Saffron put his finger to his lips. "Shh," he said softly. "OK, girls and boys. The curtain is about to rise. As soon as it has risen all the way, we will begin our song."

"I am nervous, Tammy," Terri whispered. Her mouth felt dry. "What if we forget the words? What if I forget the words to my solo?"

"We will not forget," said Tammy, as the curtain rose slowly.

"Quiet now," whispered Mr Saffron. He raised his hands in the air. Then he brought them together. And the choir began its song.

Terri peeped over Mr Saffron's shoulder at the audience. The audience seemed to stretch for ever. A sea of faces. Terri looked for her parents. She could not see them in the crowd, but she knew they were there.

Terri began to relax. The choir finished "Where Have All the Flowers Gone?" with Max's solo. Then they sang another song, the one with Kate's solo. When they finished, Mr Saffron grinned at them. Then he turned around. Mrs Titus, the head, was walking across the stage. She stopped in the middle and faced the audience.

"Good morning," she said. "Welcome, parents, teachers and pupils. And welcome to our special guests from Burger Town. As you know, our pupils have been very busy with their readathon."

Mrs Titus explained how the readathon had worked. Finally she said, "And now, I have wonderful news. At the end of the last day of the readathon, our caterpillar was four hundred and forty-eight links long. That means that our pupils have read one hundred and twelve *thousand* pages."

Terri heard some of the people in the audience gasp.

Mrs Titus smiled. "Very impressive," she said. "And a hundred and twelve thousand pages earned eleven thousand two hundred dollars for our library."

The audience clapped.

A man stepped on to the stage. He walked to Mrs Titus.

"Meet Henry Coles," said Mrs Titus. "He is from Burger Town. Mr Coles, thank you so much for coming. And thank you for giving our school the chance to hold the readathon."

"My pleasure," said Mr Coles. He gave a short speech. And then he handed Mrs Titus a cheque.

After that, Mrs Titus announced the winners of the prizes. Mrs King's fourth-graders won the prize for the class that read the most pages. They were given a set of books called *The Chronicles of Narnia*. Then one pupil in each class won a prize, too.

Terri listened to hear Mrs Titus say, "And in Miss Colman's class . . ." When she did, Terri squeezed her eyes shut.

"And in Miss Colman's class, the winner is Tammy Barkan."

"Yes!" cried Terri.

Mrs Titus handed the prize to Tammy. It was gift-wrapped. Tammy would have to open it later.

A few minutes later, Terri heard Mrs Titus say, "Thank you again, Mr Coles. From all of us. Now our choir will sing one last song. Mr Saffron?"

Mr Saffron raised his hands. Terri and

her friends began to sing "Tomorrow" from the show "Annie".

Terri sang the second verse by herself. She heard her voice ring out loudly. She was proud of herself for singing the solo, proud of Tammy for winning the prize, and proud of herself *and* Tammy for having the courage to be different.